"An engaging, creative, fascinating, and unusual mix of storytelling highly recommended for elementary age children."

~Virginia Carlson,
Children's Coordinator Penrose Library, Pikes Peak Library District

Dreams are like the paints of a great artist. Your dreams are your paints; the world is your canvas. Believing is the brush that turns your dreams into a masterpiece of reality.

—Anonymous

Conefarell!

The Night the

MOON ATE My ROOM!

Published by Tate Publishing & Enterprises, LLC
127 E. Trade Center Terrace | Mustang, Oklahoma 73064 USA
1.888.361.9473 | www.tatepublishing.com

Tate Publishing is committed to excellence in the publishing industry. The company reflects the philosophy established by the founders, based on Psalm 68:11,
"The Lord gave the word and great was the company of those who published it."

Book design copyright © 2012 by Tate Publishing, LLC. All rights reserved.
Cover and interior design by Elizabeth M. Hawkins
Illustrations by Jesse Blythe DeFriese

Published in the United States of America

ISBN: 978-1-62024-174-5
1. Juvenile Fiction / Social Issues / Emotions & Feelings
2. Juvenile Fiction / Social Issues / General
12.06.14

The Night the

MOON ATE My ROOM!

by Jesse Wilson

tate publishing
CHILDREN'S DIVISION

For Autumn.

ACKNOWLEDGMENTS

A special thanks to my parents and the entire Wilson-Granat family, Christopher Goffard, the Goffard girls, the Helling clan, Alan, and Ms. Brown. Thank you to all of my students. Finally, this book would not be made possible without the unwavering love, patience, and humor of my beautiful wife, Branda. Something I said when I was a kid applies here: "I love you, infinity times ten."

Table of Contents

Foreword

The stories in this book represent works that Jesse performs in front of audiences of all ages. By using masks, theatrical representations, and music, he transports students to a place where they can vividly imagine the wonderful stuff of dreams, star-stealing pirates, and magic orchestras.

This book and the work that Jesse does with children is especially meaningful to me because it represents the very real necessity for integrating the arts into education. The inherent value of creative thinking is not only the subtext of the stories in this collection, but it also defines the work that Jesse does as a professional teaching artist.

We know that, given the power and freedom to explore the creative process in a thoughtfully structured setting, children can transfer those skills to any kind of learning, both in school and in the "extracurriculars" of life. Having children learn by rote is quickly becoming a thing of the past, as educators at all levels are embracing the need to educate children for the twenty-first century. We need to teach kids how to approach a problem from multiple perspectives, to tolerate diversity of thought, to collaborate effectively, and to come up with random, unique ideas that might just work.

I'm a firm believer that bringing the arts into everyday teaching and learning is not only an excellent vehicle for school reform, but it's also more fun for everyone! The lessons in this book are varied and great, but, overall, this book teaches the value and importance of being able to pursue your dreams in the unique manner that's right for you. I am certain that *The Night the Moon Ate My Room!* will delight children, their parents, and teachers, too, as it most certainly has done for me.

~Michelle Shedro
Education Director,
Think 360 Arts Complete Education
www.think360arts.org

Prologue

I started playing the violin for my class today, but I forgot the music. I mean, it just wouldn't come to me!

Everyone laughed at me.

I tried playing the music again… they laughed even harder.

I walked off the class stage, I was so embarrassed.

On my way home, I told myself I would never, ever, play the violin, ever again.

It was the worst day of my life.

I was so angry, I punished myself. I decided not to eat my own dinner.

"Eat!" Mom said.

"Eat!" Dad said.

"No!" I said. "I stink. I'm the world's worst violinist!"

"I was just about to ask, how did the recital go?" Dad asked.

"Awful!" I said. "Worse than awful!" I marched myself up to my own bedroom without even saying good night to Mom and Dad and slammed the door shut.

I couldn't sleep, I was so angry. I stayed angry for a very long time…

It felt like it was really late at night. I stared up at the stars. Or where the stars should have been, because there weren't any. It wasn't even foggy out. That was kind of weird. But the moon was bright and full that night, bigger than I could ever even remember it.

Maybe because it was moving towards me…

Was I going out of my mind?

It kept moving towards me, getting bigger and bigger…

The moon kept coming, getting bigger and bigger… and bigger… and BIGGER… Oh man, was that moon huge! And then, craters and all, it was right in front of my window.

It just floated in front of the window, staring at me. I stared back at the moon, my mouth as open and as wide as the moon. Suddenly, the moon began to shake and quiver… then, like a volcano about to erupt, it opened its giant moon mouth. Instantly, light poured out of the moon's mouth into my room. Squinting

17

from the light, I saw that it had huge, jagged moon rocks for teeth. *This is it,* I thought. *It's been a nice life on this planet until now... Goodbye Mom and Dad...* Like a vacuum cleaner switched on, my entire room slowly rolled into the moon's mouth... Gulp!

The moon ate my room whole!

I shut my eyes tightly, too scared to breathe. Well, now I was a goner.

A few minutes passed. Opening my eyes, peeking over the covers, I saw my entire bedroom sparkling white. Like taking a bath without the water, I was in a world of warmth. I felt tingly all over. I couldn't see anything except for the glinting moonlight. Once my eyes adjusted to the brightness, I looked out my bedroom window... From the inside of the closest moon crater, I saw that I was flying,

19

flying above my home… far above the city… above the dark clouds… Flying, flying… Now, I was looking down at the face of the Earth. I knew you couldn't breathe in outer space, but for some reason, I could breathe just fine inside my room… inside the moon.

Inside the moon, I saw a lot of insides of other craters and discovered they were like telescopes, and that's when I saw the close-up views of other people sleeping inside their bedrooms. When I looked longer at them, I was able to look inside their dreams… It was like looking inside a ton of paintings at a museum. Many dreams were beautiful, and many were scary.

Suddenly, the moon spoke to me. "How ya doin'?"

"Fine," I replied. "Uh… How are

you?" I mean, what are you supposed to say to the moon after it eats your room? The moon sounded friendly enough, though. That was a relief. Its voice was big and echoey, but only because it was really big in there. Mainly, its voice sounded cool. It sounded like a friend.

The moon said, "You don't seem fine."

"Well… I guess I'm not," I said.

"Why?"

The words just burst out of me. "Well, I played my violin horribly in Ms. Fletcher's class, and I'd been practicing forever and I sounded awful, and everyone laughed at me. I'm a failure."

"Well, I can certainly see why you're so angry," the moon said. "But did you know that some of the greatest things in life come from what you call 'failure?' How would you like to hear some stories that might make you feel better about playing the violin again?"

"Sure," I said, although I was pretty sure I wasn't ever going to play the violin again. (I couldn't possibly imagine saying "No" to the moon. That would have been rude.)

"Long before you were born, I've been up in the sky, watching... Many things have happened on this planet, and I've seen it all," the moon explained. "If you think about all the people in the world, at one time or another, they have looked at me. It's a neat thought, if you really think about it."

It occurred to me that the moon had been there for a pretty long time and that it probably knew what it was talking about.

I'm positive that everybody in history has looked at the moon.

Dinosaurs have roamed beneath the moon.

Great battles have been fought beneath the moon.

Symphonies, plays, operas, and ballets have been performed beneath the moon.

People have laughed and cried beneath the moon.

"I've always been up here," the moon said. "I've also been here when pirates flew across the night sky instead of the sea, you know… "

"What?!" I exclaimed. That really got my attention.

"Oh yeah," the moon said. "I've lived in real and dream worlds. I've also been here when strange, winged creatures lived on other planets. I've been here when

23

lonely galaxies yearned for the majestic beauty of other galaxies. I've been here when a painter saw his future in a blank canvas, and I've been here when a boy thought he would never dream again. Do you have any idea who that might be?"

I didn't say anything. Of course, I knew who that was.

Shining on the wall now, I saw the images of lot more people. And do you know what? They were behaving very childishly. I saw painters angrily destroying their paintings! I saw writers throwing their writing out their windows! I saw musicians smashing their instruments to smithereens (I could relate to that one—I wanted to do that to my stupid violin). I saw people who wrote music (they were called composers) tear up their music.

It actually was sort of funny. I saw a lot of people doing a lot of very silly things. But then, in one flash on the wall, I also saw all these people turn their anger into symphonies, plays, operas, and ballets...

And now on the wall, I saw audiences laughing and crying and clapping their hands beneath the moon.

"Imagine if all those artists had given up because they were angry," the moon said.

I didn't say anything, but I thought that was pretty cool.

"More?" the moon said.

"Sure," I said. I really did want to see more. I wasn't just saying that to be nice to the moon.

"All those people you see on your wall had dreams," the moon said. "Your dreams are always inside you. Even if

25

you can't see them, your dreams are still there. Whether you remember them or not. Just like me, the moon. But the older we get, the harder it is to remember our dreams are still there. We forget that they are the greatest things in us… "

And that's when the moon shared with me its first story.

The Star Pirates

Night after night, from his bedroom window, the boy watched the sky getting darker…

And darker…

And darker…

Until he was convinced the stars were disappearing.

He paid close attention to the world around him, too, and was now absolutely sure why nobody was lifting up their heads and gazing at the night sky.

The stars were missing. He was sure of it.

All he could do was stare at the sky, helplessly, and watch the stars disappear, one by one.

One night, he thought he saw a strange object floating up into the darkest sky he'd ever seen. He crawled outside his bedroom window and went far out into his yard for a better look, to find out what that object in the sky might be. When it got close enough, he realized what it was: a pirate ship!

He could hear them up there—pirates cackling and laughing and making awful pirate sounds. He realized what they were doing now. They were stealing the stars right out of the night sky. One by one, plucking them out of the dark, night sky, and shoving them into the belly of their ship.

The boy had to do something— quick—before all the stars in the sky disappeared because of those terrible pirates.

He climbed up a giant tree, and when the pirate ship was close enough, he leapt up in the air, grabbed hold of the ship, and climbed aboard to safety.

Oh, the terrible, awful things those pirates said as they plucked and stuffed those stars, one by one, into the pirate ship.

"Imagine how rich we'll be when we give all these stars to the Dream Thief!"

"We'll finally get our treasure!"

"We'll be richer than we ever were before!"

And they even sang a special pirate song about stealing the stars:

"We are the star stealers, yes we are! We are the star stealers… Yarr! Yarr! Yarrrrr!"

The boy couldn't take it anymore.

"They're not yours!" he shouted.

Suddenly, he realized he'd made a very, very big mistake. All the pirates were now staring at him, gnashing their ugly teeth.

"Let's tear him limb from limb, mateys!" they shouted.

"Let's throw him overboard!"

"He won't steal arrr treasure!"

They chased the boy up and down the pirate ship; they grabbed and lunged at him, but the boy was so small he kept slipping through their clutches like a tiny mouse. He scampered down a steep ladder, down… down… into the belly of the ship.

He could hear the pirates up there, looking everywhere for him. As he searched for a safe place to hide among all the gold and rubies and fancy necklaces and stolen treasure, he heard a voice saying, "Hide in here… "

He peered into the darkness. The voice was coming from a gigantic barrel. A strange glow was coming from inside it. He realized that strange glow was the stars from the night sky all crammed in together.

The boy climbed inside.

The first thing he realized was the stars weren't stars at all. Not like they appeared when he looked up at them in the night sky. The stars were beautiful, different shapes that kept turning and moving, as if from a gentle, invisible touch—as light as the wind—and they were filled

33

with many different colors: blues, greens, violets, and reds. The boy could scarcely believe it. Things were happening inside the stars that made him so excited. Out of the swirling colors, he saw paintings come to life. He saw actors performing. He saw dancers leaping into the air. He saw athletes competing—runners tearing off at blinding speeds, gymnasts flying effortlessly above a sea of staring eyes. His entire body was tingling.

They spoke to him now, in a soft, musical language he knew he'd heard somewhere before… in his own dreams.

"We're the dreams you dream your entire life! You must put us back into the night sky! You must put us back so that others may look up, see us there, and dream again!"

"But how can I? I'm just one boy!

Against all those pirates! They'll tear me from limb to limb!"

"We have a plan!" the stars said.

"Yeah? Please, tell me!"

"Wait until they sleep," the stars said all together. "Then climb up to the front of the ship, face the empty sky, and wait."

"What'll happen?" the boy asked.

"Trust us," the stars said.

"Okay... " Who was he to argue with a barrel full of stars?

So the boy waited. He was nervous. It felt like forever as he waited inside the barrel of stars.

And then... it was time to make his move. He crept outside, among the sleeping, awful pirates. He tiptoed to the front of the ship. There, he faced the empty night sky, just as he was told to do. He waited...

35

Suddenly, he heard something very strange! Could it be…? It was the pirates. Whimpering… then whining… then sniffling. They began bellowing and howling, as if shaken from their sleep. They began crying, "Mamma! Mamma!"

The boy could scarcely believe his ears: pirates wanting their mommies? But he didn't complain. This was much better than being thrown overboard or torn limb from limb.

"What would you have us do?" the pirates exclaimed with terrible fear in their eyes. They were asking… him.

The boy thought of the only thing he wanted.

"Put the stars back!" he said.

"Of course!" they said. "Right away!"

The Pirates formed a line down into the galley and scooped up the stars from the gigantic barrel. Then, one by one, they put the stars back into the night sky, without so much as a single complaint. It was for real. They weren't trying to trick him at all. They were scared. Imagine that—scared pirates!

Already, the night sky was brighter, and the boy was very happy and proud. As he sailed home on the ship through the glowing sky, among the strangely peaceful pirates, he had to wonder, just what, actually, had happened? How and why had the pirates changed?

With his home in sight, he heard, or rather, felt inside him, the stars in the sky speaking to him again.

"Even pirates dream," they said so softly. "And sometimes they become bad dreams. They become nightmares. We filled their pirate minds with such terrible thoughts and such terrible sounds that they begged us to stop! We said, 'Listen to the boy and do exactly what he says, and if you don't, you'll all turn into gazlookas! The ugliest gazlookas you've ever seen!' Well, if you believed that would happen, you'd do anything, right?"

"Right," the boy said, but really, he had no idea what gazlookas were, though he was certain they probably weren't very nice things to ever look at. He had to ask, though, because he was very curious. "What are they?"

"Gazlookas are creatures that can't dream," the stars said. "The Dream Thief rests on people's imaginations like a thick blanket and swallows their dreams whole. And before they know it, those poor people are gazlookas. Nobody really knows to what purpose the Dream

Thief does this. But gazlookas do, from morning till night, is slowly walk around in circles in a dreamless world. Anything and anyone can become a gazlooka when the Dream Thief strikes!"

The boy shivered, thinking about becoming a gazlooka.

"But do you think they'll go back to being the mean pirates like they were before?" the boy asked.

"Probably," the stars said with a sigh. "But maybe next time, when they decide to steal something, they'll think twice about taking stars. They'll be afraid we'll turn them into gazlookas!"

The boy climbed down the rope ladder from the pirate ship into his warm, cozy bedroom. He was very happy to be back.

From his bedroom window, he

39

watched the pirate ship sail away into the night sky. He now saw the stars shining more brightly than he'd ever seen them before! Over the next few nights, he noticed more and more people starting to look up at the night sky. And he could almost hear their dreams showering down upon them as they lifted their heads up to the sky, gazing once again at the shimmering sea of stars.

He knew why, but he decided to keep that secret to himself.

The Birds and the Stars

The warmth of the sun bathed every inch and corner on the planet that knew no night. The creatures, the flowers, and the trees on the sun planet only knew what it was to live joyfully under the blazing embrace of the sun. On the sun planet, there was a dance, filled with a million swirling colors, and within those colors there arose the chorus of endless birdsong.

43

On the sun planet, there lived the most incredible-looking birds you could ever imagine. The colors of their wings that reflected against their sleek, swift bodies were dream-like colors. The red bird was the most beautiful red, and the green bird was the most beautiful green, and so was the yellow bird, and the violet bird, and the blue-pink-red-violet bird, and the polka dot bird—yes, there was even a polka dot bird. Thousands and thousands of birds with incredible and extraordinary colors.

The birds lived in harmony, singing peacefully with every breath and flap of wing they took, until one day... the red bird noticed something. He was down at the huge birdbath where everybody was drinking. *Why hadn't I noticed it before?* the red bird thought to himself. He saw the reflection of the green bird next to him and noticed that she was... different from him. Just a simple observation spread like a wildfire when that red bird said, so simply, "Hey, you're different from me!"

Overhearing this, the yellow bird looked at the bird next to him, the violet bird, and said, "Hey, you're different from me!" Then, all of the other birds noticed, too—all the birds were different from one another. At once, they said, "Hey, you're different from me! You're different from me! You're different from me! You're different from me!"

Across the entire planet, the birdsong stopped. A new sound fell across the air: silence. They stared at each other. It was true... The red bird was different from the violet bird, the violet bird was different from the yellow bird, the yellow bird was different from the green bird, the green bird was different from the blue-pink-red-violet bird, and the polka dot bird certainly was more different than the other birds. Thinking to himself, he thought, *Wow. I really am different!*

Curiosity turned into fear, which turned into anger. Instead of accepting these obvious differences between one another and going back to their bird-song, they began to fight.

It was a terrible fight. Their once soft, musical voices had now been turned into the sound of screeching pain. Their fighting might have gone on forever when, suddenly, a huge shadow stretched over the entire planet. They'd never seen anything like this before.

The huge shadow belonged to one

single, incredibly large owl whose feathers were filled with colors they'd never imagined before: very dark colors... the colors of night.

The great owl spoke in a big, booming voice, saying, "Find a way to overcome your differences, or else you shall know more of my powerful shadow!"

The birds, trembling in fear below the shadow of the great owl, could barely utter the words: "We're very sorry! We won't ever fight again! We promise!"

After several moments hovering in the sky, the great owl flew away...

For the next few days, all the birds tried to make their lives the same as it was before. But their singing was forced now, strained. Their world was... different. This time, now that they were used to seeing how different they were from each other, they really noticed they were different from each other. More than just their colors, they discovered that other birds had weird designs and patterns within their colors. They also noticed their bodies were shaped differently than the others, that other birds didn't fly as fast as the others, and that some of their voices really stuck out differently from the others when they tried to sing together as before.

"What kind of things are those on that bird's body?"

"Circles or squares?"

"It's bad enough that he flies like that, but did you hear his voice? Terrible! Terrible!"

All these arguments, and more, seemed to be a good enough reason to begin fighting again.

This time, the fight was even worse than before. It was a battle. Many birds lost their lives in the battle. The battle might have gone on forever if it wasn't for the enormous shadow that stretched over the planet again.

All the birds trembled in fear as the owl reached into the depths of its profound darkness, took hold of a giant, dark blanket, and flung it far and wide across the sky, casting the sun-filled bird planet in complete and total darkness.

The birds below begged and pleaded with the great owl to take the blanket away, but no answer came. The great owl had already disappeared. All that remained was the dark blanket in the sky.

The birds couldn't move; they were so scared.

"What's happened to our world?"

49

"I can't move!"

"I can't see my wings!"

Days passed… The birds were so hungry, but they couldn't see to find food. They had to figure something out—and fast—before they all starved to death. One thing they could all agree on: the blanket had to disappear if they were to survive.

At first, a few brave birds took to the sky to tear the blanket down. Very quickly, however, they realized that the blanket was much farther up than they even imagined, and they fell in exhaustion back to the ground. The next group of birds tried to do the same thing, and failed. The third group tried the long flight, but the exact same thing happened to them as well. Flying was useless.

"What now? What now?" the birds cried out in the darkness.

Finally, one bird in the crowd of terrified birds had another idea. "Why don't we climb?"

"Climb? Have you lost your mind? We're birds! We don't climb!"

Other birds laughed, hearing such a crazy idea. "What are we supposed to climb on? How are we supposed to get up there?"

Instantly understanding, a bird shouted, "Why don't we use each other!"

After much grumbling among the birds, another bird said, "What choice do we have?"

Another voice rose up from the darkness and said, "Let's climb while we still have energy left!"

"You mean on top of each other?"

"Yes! Like a ladder!"

"How utterly ridiculous!"

"Why? Let's try it!"

"What choice do we have?"

Awkwardly, the birds began to climb on top of each other. It was true: birds were not meant to climb on top of each other. But as one bird said—it didn't appear as if they had a choice.

"Ouch! Watch your wings!"

"Your beak is poking me!"

"Move it! Don't stop!"

"I'm falling!"

"No you're not! I'll help you!"

"Keep climbing!"

They didn't stop climbing. They climbed and kept climbing for days… and days… and days. And when one bird on top of the bird ladder got tired, another bird from below took over, and then another, and then another, and then another.

Finally, they arrived.

The blanket was much bigger than they thought it would be. It might as well have been another planet they were facing. Still, the birds began to dig their sharp beaks into the thick darkness. They began to peck and prod and finally poke their beaks through.

Tiny, thin, little lines of light began to shine through the blanket now—one after another, more and more little lines of light began to shine through. The holes of light grew to the thousands, but the birds couldn't hold on any longer. The giant ladder began to buckle and shake.

"Watch out!"

"I'm slipping!"

"Help me!"

"I can't hold on!"

The ladder of birds collapsed. Thousands of birds covered the dark planet. Beyond exhausted, under the cold blanket above them, they instantly fell into a deep, dreamless sleep.

After what felt like days had passed, they awoke, covering their tiny eyes with their colorful wings. Sunlight had burst upon the entire planet again! The blanket was gone! Had they been dreaming? It was too good to be true! They ate heartily. They played in the water. They laughed. They danced. A party like they'd never had before began—a wild, colorful party filled with laughter and rejoicing for the warm, wonderful, bright sun. The birdsong rose from their throats. It felt like eternity since it filled the air. The birds spread their wings, soaking up the hot, welcoming warmth of the sun, and the dance of colors began again. The dance might have gone on forever when the enormous shadow of the great owl appeared. Its wings stretched over the earth. The birds below trembled in fear.

The owl spoke. With its huge, booming voice, it said, "The blanket was never meant to be torn down but to be used as a reminder for the days when you shall notice even more differences beyond your own wonderful colors—and for that reason alone, this blanket will appear once during the day."

The birds were happy just to have the sunlight appear—anything was better than total darkness again.

From that moment on, just as the great owl had promised, the days were half-filled with light and half-filled with darkness. In time, the birds discovered that they began to love the dark blanket as much as they loved the light, for those tiny little holes they'd made with their sharp beaks were really quite beautiful. Twinkling and shimmering in the blanket, it reminded them all of when they became a ladder and climbed to the sky, the day they created the stars together.

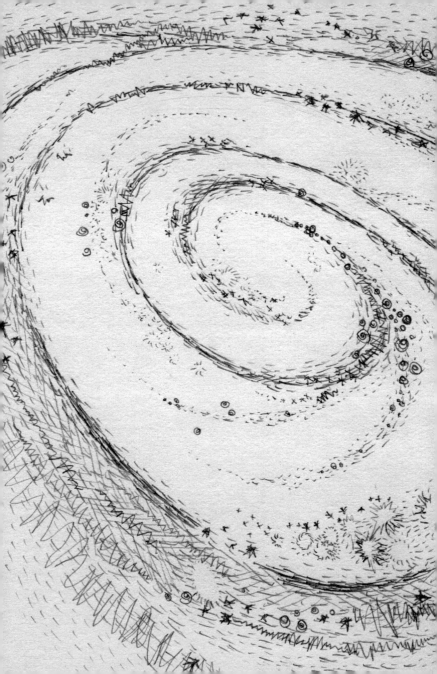

The Smudge

If you take a white crayon and then smear it on a piece of black paper, and then take your thumb and smear it in, that's what the Smudge looked like in the night sky.

Or so it thought…

Deep into the night sky lived the Smudge. The Smudge was very lonely. There was no one to talk to up there.

The one thing it could do very well was see. It had an amazing talent at being able to look far and wide into distant galaxies, but this also felt like a curse to the

Smudge because it spent light-years comparing itself to those other galaxies—those other galaxies that were filled with the most incredible colors and shapes. Some galaxies were disk-like marvels of light, while others spiraled into themselves like glittering seashells. Every galaxy the Smudge looked at was magnificent and original, in comparison to what the Smudge thought of itself. Almost every day, the Smudge would sigh a huge sigh of sadness, and it wished—oh how it wished—to be like those other beautiful galaxies. They were so beautiful, sometimes it made the Smudge want to burst into tears just looking at them. The Smudge couldn't stop staring at them. It looked at those galaxies, at all their delicious, swirling colors, and the more it longed to be like them, the more it became disgusted with itself. The Smudge would cry and sigh and say to itself, all alone up in the dark night sky, "I am just a lonely Smudge with not one thing to talk to… How I wish I could be like those other beautiful things so far away from me. But I am all alone. I am just a lonely, lonely, ugly smoosh of nothingness, a blur, a wobbly bunch of nothingness! An ugly… Smudge!"

The Smudge was wrong, of course. That's not really what it was…

One day, the Smudge was again staring at those beautiful galaxies swimming with colors so far away from itself and was sighing with sadness, murmuring, "I am just a lonely Smudge with nobody to talk to… How I wish I could be like those beautiful things. But instead, I am just a very lonely, very sad, very ugly, Smudge…"

Then the Smudge heard a small voice, crying, from inside itself. The Smudge had spent so long looking at other distant galaxies it seemed almost impossible to look inside itself now. After a moment, it was able to see that the voice was coming from a very sad, very lonely planet whose name was Thea. Thea was, in fact, crying—just like the Smudge.

"Why are you crying?" the Smudge said to the planet named Thea.

"Who's talking to me?" Thea said in disbelief. "I must be going crazy!"

"I must be going crazy, too," the Smudge said. "What am I doing talking to you?"

Thea started to really cry now. "You

had to rub it in, didn't you? I know I'm small, I'm worthless…"

"That's not what I meant," said the Smudge.

But Thea was so consumed with her own sadness that she wasn't listening. The planet was filled with fear. She wailed with tears: "I have no idea where I came from, and I don't even know where I'm going. I'm all alone in this cold blackness! I'm so afraid! I'm nothing!"

"Don't say that," the Smudge said. "You're not nothing!"

"Easy for you to say," Thea answered. "Why you… you're incredible!"

"Me? A Smudge? An ugly smoosh of nothingness?"

Hearing the Smudge say that, Thea couldn't help but laugh.

Thea said, "Don't you know who you

really are? You're not a Smudge at all. You're something far greater than that…"

"I am?" the Smudge said with wonder. "Please tell me… What am I?"

"I really don't know what exactly you are, but I know you're more important than me," Thea said.

"How sad," the Smudge said. "We both don't know who we are."

The Smudge and Thea shared their friendship with each other for a few light-years or so until one day, something happened. "Thea!" the Smudge cried. "Something's happening to you! You're… spinning!"

"What's happening?" Thea said. "What! What is it? Tell me! Please!"

Thea couldn't see what was happening to herself, but the Smudge could. It almost didn't want to tell Thea, but

Thea made the Smudge tell her. Finally, the Smudge said, "Thea, you're heading directly toward another planet!"

"Wh-what? What do you mean?" Thea cried. "I can't see it! Where? Where is it?"

Thea, indeed, was moving faster and faster, picking up speed toward a planet that millions of years later would be named Earth.

"Any day now you should see it," the Smudge said. "Like I do."

"I'm scared," Thea said.

"I know," the Smudge said. "I am too."

Finally the day had arrived.

"I see it!" Thea said. "I see it! Oh no, it's… enormous!"

Thea was right. Planet Earth was

much bigger than Thea. About nine times bigger than Thea to be exact.

"Don't leave me," Thea begged the Smudge. Gravity had tied itself around Thea like a rope.

"I won't. I promise. I'm here," the Smudge said.

All the Smudge could do was watch its friend hurtling faster and faster toward Earth.

"You're the only friend I've ever had," Thea said. "Thank you for being with me all this time… "

"You're the only friend *I* ever had," the Smudge said. "Thank you for being with me."

Thea was now minutes away from colliding into Earth. Helplessly, the Smudge watched Thea smash into the planet. She tore into Earth, chucking a ginormous chunk of Earth's crust out into space. Thea was beyond recognition. Thousands and thousands of rocks floated into space and began to slowly form their own orbit around Earth… and Thea disappeared.

The Smudge was terribly sad and alone again. Its only friend was gone.

It was not long before the Smudge went back to looking outside itself, staring longingly at other distant galaxies again, wishing for a better "life." The Smudge felt terribly sorry for itself. And then one day, as it was crying and sighing, saying, "I am just a lonely Smudge without anyone to talk to," the Smudge heard a familiar voice calling him.

"Hey, friend!"

"Who's that?" the Smudge said.

"It's me. It's Thea!"

"What? Is that really you, Thea?" the

Smudge said, so happy to hear its friend's voice again. "Where are you?"

"Look inside!" Thea shouted.

"Where?"

"Here! I'm next to planet Earth!"

The Smudge realized the voice was coming from a small, crater-covered planet orbiting the Earth. It was coming from the moon.

The Smudge noticed something else that was new, too. The Earth was filled with color! It was covered with trees and oceans and clouds and rainbows. It was filled with life. The Smudge couldn't believe all this had happened while it was spending so much time looking at other galaxies again.

"I thought you were gone," the Smudge said. "I thought I would never see you again!"

"No… I just became a part of something greater. If it wasn't for me, there may not be any life on Earth. All those colors… I'm a part of a hundred different pieces of rocks now. Some are from me. Some are from Earth. They're my family. Just like you're my family. And if it weren't for you, the Earth and the moon wouldn't exist. Finally, I know where I belong. I'm home."

Over time, with Thea's help, the Smudge was able to spread its powerful gaze to other things, now, inside itself… It started looking farther. The Smudge discovered other planets of all sizes. And more planets. And more planets. And stars! So many stars! An ocean of stars. Just like planet Earth, they were inside the Smudge the whole time. The Smudge was happier than it had ever been. After

69

that, it was no longer alone, because now it had so many beautiful things inside itself to discover for a million years… and maybe even a lot longer than that.

The Smudge was finally home… where it had always been.

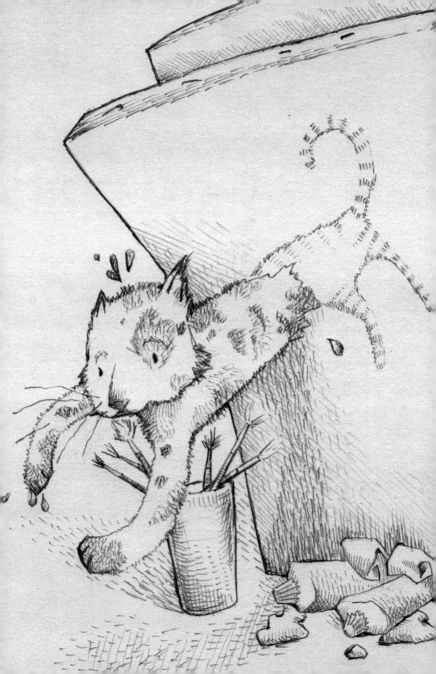

Junkyard Bob

The very old man wore a white cowboy hat, blue sunglasses, and had a scraggly gray beard. All his life, he'd collected junk in an old school bus he once bought from nearly a lifetime of giving away junk. As he was setting up for his latest junkyard, a beat-up truck drove over the hill in the distance. At the junkyard, the truck rolled to a stop. The painter got out and began to look around.

At his last and final art show in the city, just like all the other shows that came before it, not one single painting of the painter's was ever sold. The gallery owner, whose job it was to sell art to the public, decided to stop selling the painter's art.

"What can I do if no one wants to buy your paintings?" the gallery owner said to the painter.

When the painter had returned to his tiny studio, he looked at his paintings with disgust.

"These are the ugliest paintings in the world!" the painter shouted. "I hate my paintings! It's no wonder no one wants to buy my paintings! Why can't I be a famous artist like Monet or Picasso?"

He began to destroy his own paintings.

In the midst of his anger, a filthy,

skinny cat appeared on his windowsill, crying out in hunger.

"Go away," the painter said. "I have nothing to give you."

The cat leapt from the windowsill into the painter's small studio. "Go away!" the painter shouted.

Startled by the painter's anger, the starving cat scrambled onto a loose shelf and ended up dumping several cans of paint all over itself. "Oh no, look at all my paint on the floor!" the painter said. "Ahh, what does it matter? Nothing good will come from that paint anyway." He was so miserable that he forgot about the poor cat that was covered, whiskers to tail, in fresh paint. Sadly, with a line of colorful paw prints following him, the cat jumped back onto the windowsill and disappeared into the night.

The next day, the painter got in his truck and moved to the desert. He lived in a small house out in the middle of this huge, sandy nowhere. He tried to tell himself that he was happy being completely alone; but in time he began to feel lonely. He missed the company of people around him. Deep down inside, he wished he could paint again, beautifully as he once had many years ago before he thought about being a famous painter.

One day, feeling more lonely than ever, he decided to go for a drive and he happened upon a small sign off the side of the road. It said: "Junkyard, one mile ahead." Curious, the painter turned onto the dirt road and headed toward the junkyard, expecting to see people buying and selling things like most junkyards. But there was no one in sight.

He got out of his truck now and walked around, looking at all the junk displayed. He saw a dusty mirror. A rusty trombone. A rickety writing desk. As he was looking at a bunch of old hats, seemingly out of nowhere, a very old man appeared out of the blinding sunlight. Even before the old man spoke, the painter sensed a friendliness so huge in him, he no longer felt like a stranger to the man.

"I'm Bob!" the old man said in a country drawl. "How are ya, young man?"

"Fine. How are you?"

"I'm doin' pretty good for an old man. It's a beautiful life, and I ain't complain' one bit. Come see the last of my goods. A lot of people have taken things away already," the old man said to him pleasantly. "Look around! If ya see anything you need, ya just holler," old Bob said. "All ya have to do is ask."

The painter walked toward what he thought was a bunch of paintings leaning against a dusty bookshelf. He approached one canvas with its back turned to him. The painter turned it around but discovered this canvas was perfectly blank. *How much does this strange old man think he can get for a blank canvas?* the painter thought to himself. He started to walk away when the frame tipped over on the ground, knocking over a bunch of other seemingly worthless items.

"Ah! You've discovered something you like!" the old man said.

"But I didn't touch—"

The old man went right on talking as if he hadn't heard the painter. "Well boy, it's yours! You may take it home with you!"

The painter didn't want to be rude and tell the old vendor there was nothing on any of those canvases he saw. As if old Bob could hear the painter's thoughts, he chuckled. "There's plenty of stuff on 'em, young fella—you just got to look a little closer."

The painter picked up the frame, and this time, when he turned the canvas around, a painting did appear! Colors began to circle, turn, weave inside and out, until he saw his own house in the desert filled with many other paintings. It was an amazing sight, and it filled the painter with an excitement he hadn't felt in so long.

"Paint, young sir," the old man said. The painter wasn't at all sure why the old man had given away this magical paint-ing for free.

"You mean… for free?" the painter asked, hoping there wouldn't be a price for it. He certainly couldn't afford it—he barely had enough money to eat.

"Sure, free!" the old vendor replied. "Don't need anything for it."

At his home the painter stood back, admiring the magic painting on the wall. He collected all his brushes, paints, his own blank canvases that he had brought from the city, and began to paint again. He tried copying the painting he got from the junkyard, and with it, images of the desert filled with the colors of his dreams. But as he did, mysteriously, the painting on the wall went blank, as white as a bed sheet! *That old man must have played an evil trick on me,* thought the painter.

Trying to remember the images of those paintings inside the magic painting, the painter began to explore the desert. There were millions of thorny cactus plants outside his home—just like in the magic painting. So he painted every cacti he could see. He discovered fantastically shaped rocks now. Desert creatures. And sunsets. And sunrises. He fell in love with the desert and forgot about trying to remember what was in the magic painting. All that mattered was that he was painting again. In his search for everything around him in the desert, he forgot about being famous and rich and all the noisy stuff that had nothing to do with what was in front of him right then. There was so much to explore.

As he was painting one day, a very strange thing occurred. The paint on his own canvas began to disappear! "Do I need glasses? Am I going blind? Could there be something wrong with my paint?" He had to see the old man for help. Right away.

The old man seemed to be expecting the painter…

"How does your new painting look on the wall?" old Bob asked curiously.

"Well, it was fine until it went blank!" the painter exclaimed. "And then my own painting disappeared."

"Hmm, that's interestin'," the old man said. "Let's see if I can lend a hand. First, did you want to know why this strange old man gave such an unusual painting away? It must be worth plenty, maybe you're askin' yourself... "

"Well, yes, I—"

"That's a wonderful question, and I'd be happy to tell ya, kind sir. It makes me feel good to do it. My greatest pleasure is helpin' somebody else to dream again. Have any idea who that might be? You see, my dreams, like the paintings, are strictly for sharin'. If ya hold onto 'em too tightly or let 'em go and think only about what you're gonna get from it, sometimes them dreams can just... disappear. They lose their magic! I've given away everythin' that meant anything to me in this beautiful life. Well... almost everythin'..." His old hand gestured to the remaining canvases. "And that's how I hold on to my dreams. How about another painting here ya might like?" the old man suggested.

The painter quickly picked up another blank canvas. Colors began to swirl, then, another painting transformed in front of his eyes! It was of a colorful cat happily napping on the edge of a bed. Both the cat and the room in the painting looked very familiar to the painter.

"Take it," Bob said. "Take it home. Oh, and be careful driving."

On the way home, a cat darted out in front of the painter's truck. Screeeccch! The truck swerved off the road, almost hitting the cat! When the painter got out of the truck, he found the cat, all skin and bones, sitting on the side of the road, yawning. "Crazy cat," the painter said. "If you knew how lucky you were to be alive… " The cat looked like it was starving. Feeling sorry for it, the painter picked him up and took him to his home in the desert.

Right away, the cat was given a bath. Most cats hate to get wet, but this one seemed to relish in the attention. Once the dirt was washed away, the painter saw how beautiful the cat really was, covered whiskers to claws in colors! Amazed by this, the painter decided to name him Vincent, after a famous artist he admired—Vincent Van Gogh.

Boy, was Vincent happy to eat! He garbled down as much food as he possibly could. The cat was incredibly happy. It jumped up on the edge of the painter's bed, curled up, and fell into a deep, cozy sleep.

As the painter hung his new painting on the wall, he suddenly realized Vincent on his bed looked… well, he was just like the cat in the painting. Something magical, indeed, was happening. But then the painting on that canvas began to disappear. And so did the actual Vincent on the bed. As the "real" cat was fading away in front of him, he could hear Vincent's thoughts saying to him, "The magic only works if you share your gift." The painter wanted that magic, the kind that Junkyard Bob had shared with him.

Quickly loading his truck with every one of his new paintings he'd made, he drove into town. The town was desolate, sad, colorless. The painter visited as many homes as he could, giving away his paintings for free. The townspeople thought the painter was crazy, but they couldn't deny how wonderful his art was. Almost instantly, the entire town was talking

about the new painter who shared his art with everyone. They all said the same thing when the painter knocked on their doors: "We have nothing to give you for it."

"Don't need anything for it," the painter would reply, cheerfully. It felt so good to give the paintings away after he'd spent so long trying to sell them in the city. But he was getting something back now. Much more than he'd ever imagined.

The beautiful colors transformed that town with laughter and happiness.

More and more color grew in that town.

It seemed as if the painter couldn't stop painting. For days and days he painted. The more he gave away, the more he painted. And the more he painted, the happier he made everyone, including himself. It was the happiest the painter had ever been in his life.

One afternoon, while busy painting, the painter saw that the last canvas old Bob had given him was changing. The colors were turning. He now saw what looked like his old studio in the city where he used to live; he saw paint splattered everywhere; and he saw the skinny, filthy cat standing on his windowsill, dripping with paint. He noticed Vincent at his feet now, looking up at the painter. "There was a time when you were worried more about the paint on the floor than a hungry cat in your window."

Suddenly, the painter remembered that day in his city studio. It felt like so long ago. "Of course! That was you, wasn't it, Vincent? Covered in paint!

How selfish I was! And you followed me all the way out here in the desert! You wonderful cat!"

He heard Vincent's thoughts in his head again: "You wouldn't be painting if it wasn't for that old man in the desert."

"How selfish of me!" the painter exclaimed. He realized he had never truly thanked Bob for what he'd been given, receiving nothing in return. He was painting again because of Junkyard Bob.

Quickly, he got into his truck and drove to see the old man.

The junkyard was gone. No one was there. There was nothing but the empty desert again. Disappointed, the painter was about to return home when he discovered a new canvas at his feet. Where had this canvas come from? He held it in his hands, waiting for a picture to emerge. But nothing happened. It remained blank.

Sometimes, a blank canvas can show us more of an actual picture than what our eyes can see. It was then the painter suddenly understood—it was up to him, the painter, to create his own future… if he was willing to share it.

With old Bob's final gift and with Vincent curled up on the seat next to him, the painter drove home, heading for his future that was already beginning to take shape.

The Dream Thief and the Magic Orchestra

The boy set the bow down on the strings of his violin. His fingers arched into position... and then... He went blank. He couldn't remember the music! His face oozing in cold sweat, his knees shaking, he tried playing again, and scccrrrrreeeeccccchhh! The worst sound he'd ever heard came out of his violin.

93

Everyone in Ms. Fletcher's fourth grade class laughed at him.

The boy had been practicing the Vivaldi from memory the night before in his cozy, safe bedroom; and that morning, ready for show-n-tell, he had it fresh in his head, but now? Gone.

For the third time, he tried playing the music—Squeeeeak, scrrraaattccchh! More horrible sounds came from his stupid violin. They laughed even harder.

Ms. Fletcher told them to stop laughing, but they didn't stop laughing until she said she'd take away their recess for the rest of their lives. That did the trick.

Still, he walked off the class stage, so embarrassed. *What's happened to me?* the boy thought to himself. *Why doesn't the Vivaldi come out the way I want it to? Why has that perfect music gone away?*

He told himself he would never, ever, play the violin ever again.

That night, he had a very strange dream…

Holding onto his violin case, the boy opened the door to Ms. Fletcher's fourth grade class. Inside, it was dark and kinda scary. The classroom seemed bigger than its normal size, too. That was sort of weird.

Suddenly, from far away, and then closer and closer, the boy heard the wailing of string instruments and out-of-tune trombones, ear-splitting oboes, and off-key clarinets! It was from an orchestra. But the strangest orchestra the boy had ever heard. *What kind of orchestra plays in the dark?* he thought. What kind of orchestra plays in a fourth grade classroom?

Despite the fearful noise, the boy walked further inside to investigate. All at once, the music came to a screeching halt. The awful-sounding orchestra stopped playing.

"Who are you? What are you doing here? Nobody invited you!" a huge voice shouted.

The voice was coming from way above the boy's head. The boy craned his neck up to the blackness and saw the awful face of the conductor glaring down at the boy from the podium he was standing on. This conductor seemed a hundred feet tall, and his skin was as white as a bed sheet.

"I'm here to play," the boy said to the conductor, barely getting the words out. "I… I play the violin. I want to play."

Why am I staying? the boy thought.

Why don't I just run out of here? I don't know why. For some reason, I have to stay...

After a few seconds, the angry conductor switched tunes and said, "Well... why not? Allow me to introduce myself... My name is Maestro Dreordius Thaddeus!" His long, rickety fingers reached toward his lapel, slowly opening his coat. "Ahh, how silly of me, I see you already have a violin!" And with his long, bony white finger, he pointed to the violin case tightly locked in the boy's hand.

In silence, the boy opened up his violin case, but instead of his old violin being there, a cloud of dust floated out, revealing another dusty, cracked violin with spiderwebs tangled around it. His own violin wasn't exactly in the best condition, but it didn't look anything like

97

this ugly thing! The orchestra's conductor had played an evil trick on the boy. Slimy bugs began scuttling and slithering out of the violin. The boy could hear the mean maestro muttering, "He'll never want this violin."

Oddly enough, the boy still wanted to play, no matter how out-of-tune the music was, and no matter how terrible this violin looked.

The boy was very surprised to find how welcome he was by the other musicians: kids who all looked to be about his age. The boys were dressed up in suits and ties and the girls wore pretty dresses, but looking closer, he could see that all their clothes were covered in dust, as if all the musicians had been sitting there for a long, long time.

Next to the boy sat a pretty redheaded

girl with dusty red pigtails and dusty freckles and a dusty, flowery dress and large, dusty glasses and dusty braces, and she was holding a violin… covered in dust.

"This is the dress I wore the day I gave my horrible recital," she whispered. "I wish I could wear another one. This dress reminds me of how awful I played on that awful day."

"What's your name?" the boy asked her.

"My name is Lyric."

"That's a cool name," he said, trying to cheer her up.

"Thanks," Lyric said. "My mom and dad named me that because they wanted me to be a singer. You know… like the lyrics to a song? But I can't sing. I really can't play the violin either. I mean, I thought I could until I gave that awful recital." All of a sudden, a line of tears streamed down her dusty, freckled face as she remembered the day she gave that performance.

"Hey, don't cry," the boy told her. "I'm sure you play the violin just fine."

"You wouldn't be saying that if you saw my recital. I totally ruined that song. And now all I do, every second, is hear myself play it… again and again."

The boy tried to change the subject so she would stop crying. "What is this strange place?" he asked her.

But she wouldn't stop crying.

"This is the room for us kids who've given bad performances and told ourselves we would never play again," a cello player named Pete said. Pete had two strings missing on his cello… They were sitting on his head like spaghetti. "It's the sound of all our bad performances together. And now all we do all day and all night is play this terrible music over and over. It won't ever stop... because of him!"

"Who is he?" the boy asked.

All the musicians whispered at once: "The Dream Thief!"

Another boy who'd once given a bad oboe performance (the reed was stuck inside his left nostril) said in a nasally voice, "I really can't stand that Dream Thief!"

"The Dream Thief?" the boy said again. What a terrible-sounding name.

"We thought you'd never show up," Lyric said, sniffing back tears. "We've been waiting for you."

"You have?"

"Way too long," Lyric said.

"But how can that be? I've never been here before!"

"You're the missing player!"

Then Lyric leaned in, whispering another secret. "You're the one who can make our orchestra play in tune again. And there's something else you didn't know about us. We're—"

Just then, their conversation was cut off by that mean orchestra conductor (a.k.a., the Dream Thief), whose face had gone from white to red now, so angry that his terrible music had been interrupted.

"Play!" he shouted. "Play my terrible, horrible, wonderful, out-of-tune-music!"

"Not again! Not again!" Lyric whimpered.

Maestro Dreordius Thaddeus whapped his baton on his metal conductor's stand, signaling the orchestra to get ready. The orchestra lifted up their instruments again and played that awful-sounding noise again.

The boy was about to join with the terrible music, and then—Pop! Snap! The strings on his violin snapped apart, one by one. Next, the violin's wooden bridge crumbled to bits. Soon the entire violin and the bow crumbled into a pile of wood at his feet.

The conductor's evil laugh echoed throughout the enormous classroom. Still, the boy summoned up the courage to announce to him, "This violin broke… Can I have another one?"

The conductor smiled down wickedly, like a giant snake with a baton.

"Do you honestly think I'd let you play with us? An outsider? Somebody to destroy my wonderfully terrible music? Now everyone, play! Play my beautifully horrible, wonderful, out-of-tune music!" Again, he whapped his baton against the stand, signaling to begin again.

Without a violin in his hands, the boy felt useless. He was about to walk away, but then something incredible happened. Instead of the awful music, there was just silence in its place. No one in the orchestra lifted up their instruments. No one played.

The conductor stomped his feet, shouting, "Play! Play my beautifully horrible, terrible, wonderful, out-of-tune music again!" This time, he whacked the baton on the stand, splintering it.

The conductor screamed with rage, demanding everyone to play his terrible music.

Then, a small voice rose up.

"Not unless he plays… " It was from Lyric, who had finally stopped crying.

The conductor stared in astonishment, uncertain about what to do.

"Him? He can't play!" he said, meaning the boy. "Why—look at him! He doesn't even have a violin!"

"Are you sure about that?" Lyric said. "Watch." She turned to the boy and asked, "Do you really want to play?"

"I guess so… "

"No, you have to be sure. Do you really want to play?"

The boy thought about it very hard. "Yes," he said, finally. "More than anything."

"I was hoping you would say that," Lyric said. "Imagine you have a violin in your hands… "

The boy pictured playing his old violin. He missed it; it was like an old friend. It didn't even matter to him what kind of sound came out of it now. Suddenly, as if seized by a magical magnet, the bits of wood on the floor from the old violin were rapidly gathering into a brand new, shining violin! This violin was so shiny that he could see the entire dusty orchestra reflected in the wood.

"Just play one note," Lyric said. "Just one."

The boy closed his eyes and played the purest-sounding note he'd ever played before. With the single note, light began to fill the huge classroom. The conductor screamed with anger, but his long, spidery legs began buckling and swaying. He demanded everyone make the terrible, out-of-tune music again, but it was far too late. And too light.

"Play again!" Lyric said to the boy.

The boy played another note. It was a magic violin! More light poured into the darkness, and just like what had happened to the first violin the boy tried to play, Maestro Dreordius Thaddeus snapped apart! His arms, his hands, his legs, and his face all collapsed into tiny pieces, settling slowly into a pile of gray dust, right on the podium. The orchestra members shouted with joy, "Down with the Dream Thief!" All together, the orchestra began to play! And… they were all in tune.

"Play again! And watch!" Lyric said.

The boy played again. Another amazing thing happened: one by one, each musician floated out of his or her seat

with the music still playing. They flew out of that classroom, up and up, above the clouds, moving farther and farther into the sky where, as he watched, they turned into stars… filling the night sky with brilliant light. There were more stars than the boy had ever seen—millions, probably.

He wanted to fly up, too. He so badly wanted to join them. *Why aren't I flying?* he thought. "I want to come up, too!" he shouted up at the stars.

Lyric, who was practically touching the clouds with her fingers, shouted down to the boy, "What are you waiting for? Just play!"

As soon as his bow glided across the strings, the boy rocketed up, far above the clouds! Below his flying feet, planet Earth grew smaller and smaller, turning into a tiny dot. Farther and farther the musicians flew, faster and faster... Just before they all turned into stars, Lyric thanked the boy.

"Why are you thanking me?" he asked her.

"When anyone decides to go for their dream, they release a world full of dreams! When you decided to play the violin, you set us free! Hey, good luck tomorrow!"

"Tomorrow? What's tomorrow?"

She started giggling. "Tomorrow, you're going to play again! You're not awake yet, silly!"

Ms. Fletcher was nice enough to let the boy play his violin again. In a weird way, when he arrived nervously in the class-room this next morning after the worst day of his life, she almost seemed to be expecting the boy to ask her to play. She seemed very happy.

For the second time, the boy set his bow across the strings of his violin, his fingers got into position, and then... he began to play. They were all out there, watching him. Even the boy's mom and dad were gathered in the classroom to come see him play again.

The Vivaldi still didn't exactly come out the way he wanted it to, but actually, that didn't matter so much now. It felt good to play the music just because he enjoyed doing it, no matter how it came out. And it really had nothing to do with being famous or having his name in lights—all the stuff he'd thought about

111

before when he was playing in his bedroom. *This is what it must feel like to really be a musician,* the boy thought. *Just sharing the music. Just playing. Just sharing… me. I'm not trying to be the world's greatest violinist, or anyone else…*

As soon as the boy finished playing, instead of laughing, Ms. Fletcher's entire class was clapping their hands, giving him a giant applause!

In the boy's dream world, he'd given a lot of great performances before, but this… this was the greatest performance of his life. It was like a dream—an amazing dream. But it wasn't, because this time, it was for real.

Epilogue

Inside a moon crater, I saw my own dream now of playing beautiful music for Ms. Fletcher's class. I didn't want to look at it really, because I knew how it would end... disastrously. While it lasted, though, the dream in the moon crater was so beautiful.

I could still hear the entire class laughing at me. All that fear came flooding back... I wanted to run away again... to disappear... The Dream Thief was real. Somehow, like a ghost, it had slipped inside the protective walls of the moon, into my bedroom, stealing my dreams.

"It's attacking me!" I shouted. "Make it stop!"

"Chill," the moon said in a very calm, but firm, voice. "You're going to need to be relaxed before I tell you the next little bit of news. I'll let you in on a secret, but don't freak out... You are the Dream Thief!"

I couldn't believe my ears. I got chills all over my arms. "What? What?! W-what do you mean?" I exclaimed. "How can I be the Dream Thief?"

"Remember, you decided that you wouldn't play the violin anymore. The Dream Thief is not some creature that lives on the outside... It lives on the inside... waiting inside you. But it can only steal from you if you let it. You leave your dreams. Your dreams don't leave you."

"Now I'm really confused."

"The best thing about being a dreamer is this: when you set your mind to making something real, even if it doesn't come out the way you plan it, it can turn into the greatest dream ever! But you have to work hard to make it come true! Let's not forget that a little persistence pays off, too. It may mean getting knocked down and occasionally laughed at. That's when the Dream Thief attacks most people, scaring them half to death! They'd rather dream than see themselves as a loser and think they have failed. It's safer to not face who you really are inside—or so most people think."

That made perfect sense to me, even if I didn't want to admit that to myself.

Still, it didn't take away the fact that I still might have to play again for real.

"Fear is just your dreams trying to test you to see if you really believe in sharing them or not. Have a ton of dreams. Someday, when you find the one you really like, one that you're daring to share outside your cozy dream world—more than just one—try it on for size. Have fun with it; wear it like a hat, explore, test it out, play! You have plenty of time, and believe me, the day will come when you'll know what you really want to do with that dream. You may realize that life can be like in a dream. Your own beautiful dream. Your own giant canvas."

I went from nervous to sad now. It was hard to tell which I felt the most. Mainly, sad. When anyone, especially the moon, says something really dramatic like that, it usually means they're mostly done talking. Which usually means that it is time for them to leave. I knew it was time for the moon to go back home.

"Okay, what's wrong now?" the moon said.

"Well, it's just that… nothing."

"I can read your thoughts, you know."

"I know. That's kind of annoying."

The moon laughed.

"Go on," the moon said. "I'm listening."

"It's just that… well, I like being here. Will I ever see you again?"

Again, the moon laughed, but not in a mean way. "You have your entire life to see me. Every night! Don't you know who I am? Hello? I'm the moon. And even if you can't see me, even on a cloudy night, I'm still here. No matter where you are. I'm here. In the night sky."

"I meant… like this," I said.

"Maybe not always like this, but every time you listen to your dreams, it's like you're talking to me," the moon said.

"Thank you."

"Don't mention it! You ready to fly back to Earth?"

"Ready."

Down from the sky flew the moon. My heart began to beat as fast as a rabbit's; my hands got cold and clammy seeing the Earth growing bigger and bigger. Back to reality. Finally, I entered the Earth's atmosphere, below the clouds. When it floated in front of my house, its giant moon mouth opened, and my room rolled out on the reverse vacuum carpet of glistening, glowing whiteness. Its huge, jaggedy moon mouth closed, and the glow was gone. The air was colder, and my arms and legs weren't tingly anymore like how they were being inside the moon.

"I'll be seeing you," the moon said.

From my bed, back in my house, I watched the moon moving away… back up… up… farther… farther… and farther away from my bedroom window, returning into the night sky. I missed being inside the moon, but it was nice to know it was there looking back at me and it would never go away. The moon would always be there, shining upon my bedroom. Shining upon my entire life.

Just before I fell asleep, like two curtains being drawn to the far right and left of the moon, the entire night sky filled, once again, with the brilliant shimmering of stars.

Tomorrow, I decided I would play the violin again.

Book the fifty-minute educational performance of *The Night the Moon Ate My Room!* at your school or arts program now! Contact www.think360arts.org

All stories in *The Night the Moon Ate My Room!* address educational and life skills with a focus on a student's valuable role with the world community.